Love Devilish Love Divine

Iris Mede & Ian Lewis

ISBN-13: 9798402889590
ISBN-10: 1477123456

Cover design by: Art Painter
Library of Congress Control Number: 2018675309
Printed in the United States of America

To Ian from Iris,
And to Iris from Ian

"Is sex dirty? Only when it's done right."
--WOODY ALLEN

Contents

Introduction

There's something for everyone in this collection of erotic poems
and stories. Among them you will find lush, romantic poetry that
can be read aloud by both partners; erotic poems that are sure
to heighten the senses and arouse primal needs; two extended
tales where lovemaking is vividly described; witty limericks sure
to bring a smile, if not a hearty laugh. In short, the collection is
very much like sex itself --stimulating, exiciting, and quite pleas-
ing. The collection can be read together between lovers or savored
individually. Either way, the collection is sure to heat up the bed.
Enjoy!

Preface

When I was growing up I was a voracious reader of erotica. However, there was a dearth of erotic reading material that was truly arousing. There was the "dirty stuff" cartoon books at the beginning that all of us, boys and girls alike, eagerly sought. But that was for shock value primarily, repetitive, and boring soon enough.

Then came the classics --*Ulysses, Lady Chatterley's Lover*, and others, but little else beyond that. My copies of those books, with all the good parts underlined, went through so many readings with sweaty hands that they were dog-eared before too long.

What I sought was something steamy, but not pornographic. Beyond innocence, there had to be a transition, a middle ground before entering the realm of the hard core. Did someone take an interest in my pubic hair beyond me? Could my feelings of what it was like to grow into a female body be described adequately? Were the experiences of other girls/women exploring their sexual parts and nature similar?
None of what I read was poetry, and none of it was written by women. That was then, and this is now.

I like to think that the floodgates have been opened. Today there are many women writers that provide a rising tide of erotic literature. We each have our distintive voices and can bring different perspectives to share what it's like to be sexually active, whether driven by lust or love.

The material in this book has been written primarily by my writing partner and lover, Ian Lewis. I edited and contributed significant portions.

My sincere hope is that this material provides pleasure and a fresh perspective to your carnal journeys, as the authors enjoyed in the flesh when they were doing their research before putting pen to paper. Our greatest joy is the gift that we all inherit, the primal experience of sex.

--Iris Mede

The First Time You Were Mine

Our hands timidly move toward
each other's hands,
across the bed and across so many,
many lonely years.

My mouth searches for your mouth,
for your tongue, your warmth
and your passion
that lie hidden and fiercely guarded.

Arms and legs stretch out and intertwine,
skin sliding on skin,
our bodies curve, turn and wrap
around each other.

Love's friction and a flood
of rushing blood turn your face
to a reddish blush, radiating heat,
primal longing and lust.

Your breasts come alive
under my gentle tongue:
nipples turn up
and follow each stroke
that grows forceful and rough.

My hand moves slowly,
ever slowly, down, down,

taking its time, lingering in spots,
moving down, down to you there.

My fingers find you:
A soft mat of hair,
a warm wetness at the very base,
dripping out, sending out
a welcome to me there.

The conversation of our bodies
carries on, conversing passion
with each stroke and touch,
each rise and fall of limb.

Your vagina and my tongue
become instant friends,
greeting and meeting the other
through the sensual language of touch.

Excitement is increasing,
flesh is now shaking and aching;
embers become fire,
stoked higher, higher and higher.

Your pelvis rises slightly
to eagerly welcome my penis
--no, it pulls, consumes
and totally absorbs it!

We move as one, yoked by passion,
driven by desire, together,
together, trembling, trembling,
trembling from so much.

We fly, we leave the bed there
and fly the night sky, flying and
circling, spying and shirking
our ordinary lives.

My penis erupts
--like it has never before,
with a spray of myself
that finds every inner part of your body.

I collapse on the bed,
we're both spent and so tired,
we talk and recollect what has transpired,
as sperm seeps out.

Our bodies are bathed
in the scents of the scene:
a musky sweet odor
that is so pungent and priceless.

Wet, motionless now,
softly breathing,
we let the earth focus
around us again and realize
that we have traveled far.

In Bed Once

In bed once you pulled on my ear
as I had my head between your thighs
and licked at your pussy.
I looked up and you had a mischievous
look on your face that I had never seen
before or since.

I carried on, more enthusiastically,
as we continued our lovemaking,
but I never forgot that.

Every once in awhile I recall that little
memory of you pulling on my ear. I don't
know why.

Among so many beautiful memories with
you I don't know why that one little thing
keeps coming back to me.

It is, though, a beautiful bit of mischief
that still lingers for me and makes me
flutter every time I think of it.

Thin White Lines

You kneel, your body enclosed in leather that I have you brought for you today. The blindfold is also leather, but more supple than the hard black leather of your halter that is connected to the black leather chaps on your legs. Otherwise, you are bare, your pussy prominently exposed.

I step forward and brush the black hair of your wig away. It falls behind you, baring the top fullness of breast, that doesn't quite fit in the studded halter top. Your chest trembles with anticipation.

I lean, and press a kiss on one hardened nipple that peeks through a triangle slit in the halter. You arch your back in semi-shock, having not expected that. (Usually I start with a kiss on the mouth.) I take in the elegant curve of your torso, with your slender arms stretched back, clasping your ankles firmly.

I start rubbing the other nipple with my right hand, while I increase the pressure of my kiss on the left. Harder and harder and harder I stroke and kiss until finally you break and the tiniest of moans escapes.

I stop.

I reach out and caress the supple whip.

Regretfully, joyfully, I anticipate the new lines that I will add to the thin, white, beautiful scars that now criss-crossing your eager body.

Our Loving

All our loving
creates motion
and makes distances
disappear;
You can travel
where you want
by just dropping
your brassiere.
In one moment
you are next to me
then the next
you're long gone;
No wonder I can't
find you here,
you're in Maui
in a bright sarong!

Spanish Boys

Spanish boys will greet you,
With an innocent refrain,
The echoes of a thousand sounds,
Of a thousand scenes the same.

But, Spanish boys will beat you,
At your own familiar games,
Their sweetness hides the cunning
Of their sexual ruse and chains.

They make better lovers,
Or so I've been told,
Under the covers,
Is where you discover if they're all that bold.

They don't come easy,
But they're worth the time,
And if you please them,
Then, maybe, they'll love you sometime.

Spanish boys are tricky,
They'll flatter you with lies,
Handle you the way you would,
But in a more demure disguise.

And Spanish boys will fool you

Into total compromise,
With only occasional candy
To keep your ego satisfied.

They make better lovers,
Or so I've been told,
Under the covers,
Is where you discover if they're all that bold.

They don't come easy,
But they're worth the time,
And if you please them,
Then, maybe, they'll love you sometime.

They say they'd never hurt you,
Because they'd only hurt themselves,
And they don't mean
To dry up all your wishing wells.

They say they should be truthful,
But something tells you they lie,
And though you know it is, the way it is,
It still tears you up inside.

They make better lovers,
Or so I've been told,
Under the covers,
Is where you discover if they're all that bold.

They don't come easy,
But they're worth the time,
And if you please them,
Then, maybe, they'll love you sometime.

Passion

She produces passion in me by her mere caress;
--Her touch is both a miracle
and yet seems so familiar.

She touches me, she teases me, she scorches me;
--Her fingers are like fire
that singe and burn.

She sears the very air from me and I can hardly breathe;
--And yet I yearn for her
firm control of all I am.

We roll and sweat on softly scented bedclothes;
--Everything seems warm
and everywhere seems wet.

I tremble as your tongue feeds to me more passion,
--And a love than seems
to capture and possess.

You are the huntress, tall and triumphant on the hill;
--Your weapon is your passion
and I am the one you kill!

The Painting

He stared at the painting for a very long time. Yes, it did look like it. It had that same crease and that same rounded dimple at the top. "Yes, of course it is," he thought to himself as he slowly nodded his head up and down, it was a fair depiction of her vagina.

They had been in the small storefront gallery for a few minutes before he spotted the painting of a flower, the painting that he now realized must have been intended to resemble the female body's most intimate body part, a woman's sexual connection to another, the delta point of her pelvis, her genitalia.

No, he couldn't be certain. It could have been intended to be a flower only. It had a central opening, which was surrounded by a "V" rise at the top and an inverted "U" at the bottom. The opening had a vertical shape, with a rounded crease at the top. It could be an unfolding pansy, or a stylized water lily. But, the earthy colors of magenta, cream and beige were unlike any botanical bloom. Yes, it was definitely a woman's genitalia! He wasn't imagining it.

But, was it her genitalia? This he could only imagine. The colors seemed right, or at least they could have been right. He had only observed her's close-up in the dim glow of candlelight. He smiled. Yes, that is what it should look like: A soft connection of lines, creases and colors. But, her's is much more vibrant than that. Her's has warmth, scent and motion. It smells like, like . . . .

Oh, she was at the far end of the gallery and motioned for him. Well, she was far more interesting than any picture of her intimate parts, he thought to himself, and so he joined her.

"Hi," he said as he approached her in the back viewing room of the gallery. She was there with a salesperson and they had a painting on the viewing wall. He took her hand as the lights in the room were slowly dimmed and then raised again. He moved to an angle that allowed him to see her crotch. She had loose fitting linen pants on. That did little to excite the imagination, he thought Still, as she and the salesperson were focusing on the painting on the wall, he stared in the direction of her crotch and imagined what might lie beneath the light-colored linen.

They left the gallery and started walking down the street in La Jolla again. He couldn't get his mind on anything else. They passed a restaurant and he quickly scanned the menu: Mushroom soup, Bibb lettuce salad, artichoke and drawn butter --they somehow remind him of her genitalia again.

They walked along on the beach path and reminders of her genitalia were everywhere: The sensuous curves of the gnarled cypress were reminders, as were the waffling scent of the massed flowers in the bedding areas. Everything, everything reminded him of her genitalia. How long will it be until they get to his place again, he wondered. Is dinner necessary? Perhaps . . . not!

The Gifts

Delicately she opened her top to me
and offered me her breasts
with her two hands
as one might offer a gift to the gods.

"Love them please and love them well,"
she said in a whisper I could barely hear.

"I love them so very much!" I replied,
"for they are many gifts to me:
They are my playthings
and I will amuse myself with them.
I will play and stay with them
for many hours both day and night.

I will give them pleasure
and they will pleasure me.
I will share with them softened marzipan
and chocolate drizzle any time I can.
Their little tips will often know my lips
and learn to love the many kisses I will give.
I will tease them often
to make them tautly aware
that as I am caressing them
I will also be kissing you."

This Day

Getting through this long day
was such sheer punishment,
knowing you would be there,
and all the things you represent.

For your body shelters
in a way I don't quite know,
and you spark and nourish
both my body and my soul.

Your lips that kiss and uplift me
are my reward for the day:
a maze filled with many phonies
and convention to be obeyed.

Your breasts are pure treasures
that wait to be mine
after I've dealt with problems
that just seem to take up time.

I hear your thighs call me,
"Hurry here," they seem to say,
"We await you in the night,
as reward for the trying day."

Limerick #1

There once was a lady vegetarian
Who said meat was for a barbarian;
That didn't stop her from taking,
The cum her love was making,
Saying, "I guess I'm also a contrarian."

Limerick # 2

There was a blond lady who complained,
That her breasts weren't the biggest, that's plain.
But they made up for their size,
By getting the prize,
For the cute looking nipples they contained!

This Morning

This morning I remembered
your breasts
on my hands
and how they curved out
slightly to each side;
eyes for nipples,
opening wide at my touch.

Wonderful

I had a wonderful night with you,
In my dreams, last night,
When everything went just right!

I was sentenced to a year
And I enjoyed it, dear,
Between your outspread legs.

I was punished by,
And I didn't even cry,
By being chained to your bed.

I could only see you,
And it was such a wonderful view,
Twenty-four hours a day.

You only wore a silk shift,
That was an easy lift,
To see you all and bare.

I was forced to have you sit
And to totally submit,
As you sat upon my face.

I had a wonderful night with you,
In my dreams, last night,
When everything went just right!

This Night

On this night I am drunk
from so many kisses,
that left your lips more mellow and fine than wine.

The stars have risen higher
than never, ever before,
and isn't it pure melted gold that the big dipper pours?

Now, high among the stars
you remove your robe,
and all the heavens glimmer to give you their applause.

Your gaze seems to rest on me
and I am without cares,
in an orbit around the most heavenly body I see --Thee!

Taming You

"What does that mean --'tame?'"

"It is an act too often neglected." said the fox. "It means to establish ties."

"To establish ties?"

"Just that," said the fox. "To me, you are still nothing more than a little boy who is just like a hundred thousand other little boys. And I have no need of you. And you, on your part, have no need of me. To you, I am nothing more than a fox like a hundred thousand other foxes. But if you tame me, then we shall need each other. To me, you will be unique in all the world. To you, I shall be unique in all the world . . . ."

--Antoine De Saint-Exupery, The Little Prince

As I picked up your clothes last night and folded them over the chair I remembered the first time I had done that; It was about six months ago. (Only six months ago? What an eternity ago that seems now.)

I took off your pants that evening and slowly, very, very slowly folded them over the back of the chair. Then, also very slowly, for the first time, my hands traveled the curves of your body: The distances seemed vast and uncharted.

I placed my two hands on the back of the small of your back and crossed the ridge line of your panties and continued down along the ridges of your hips. I felt the line that split you into two hemispheres. I brought my hands around and rotated them and found that it excited you. I brought my hands closer together just below your navel and coming around your thighs approached your vagina as it waited, dreaming of adventure.

Then everything sped up again. We had raced up, as you recall, that first night, to my bedroom after passionate, frantic kisses on the sofa. We were both eager and wild. We practically knocked into each other racing up the stairs, through the bedroom door and into bed.

Then it slowed down. Then it was like we were moving in slow motion, slowly taking our time, slowly beginning to learn each other, slowly learning what it was like being with the other.

All this was before I knew how you liked your morning coffee, how you liked to read the newspaper in the morning, before I knew how it felt to go to sleep next to you, and sleep next to you, and wake up next to you, and lie there a long time listening to you sleep.

Your Spirit

Your spirit and I made love today,
In the chambers of my mind.
We clung together passionately,
Until we exhaustedly resigned.

Someday

Someday we may not need
to touch so much
or to devour each other's bodies
with our eyes
and minds,
and in our dreams,
but now we do.

It's not easy being next to you
and having so many salacious thoughts.

--Can the waitress tell
that my mouth is at your breast
and my hand is pumping you
while I read the menu?

--Is the movie cashier aware
of what I really want to do
when we go into
that darkened theater?

It could be that time
will make it easy
to be beside you
without wanting
to be inside you,

but, maybe not.

Tell Me What

Tell me what I have to do
and tell me what I have to be,
to have you forever at my side
and to make sweet love to me.

Must I climb the highest cliff,
or swim the ocean floor?
Must I crawl over broken glass?
Do you demand that and more?

Or can you take me as I am
with all my issues and my flaws?
And can you pull me to your chest
without hesitation or a pause?

Please slide your hungry tongue
between my parted lips
and run your anxious fingers
along my quivering hips.

Wrap me in your passion,
expose your every need;
Press your steamy lips to mine,
-- every secret freed.

Sprinkle your tears across my cheek,
confess every desire
Moan my name, call me yours,

and set my soul on fire.

Need me more with every breath
that slips into your chest,
Please me nightly, miss me daily,
never compare me with the rest.

Grip my wrists; look in my eyes,
say the words I long to hear
Kiss me roughly, and weep my name,
forever hold me dear.

Do I ask, dear, for wishes
that can never quite come true?
Is my greatest sin, my fatal flaw,
that I can't stop loving you?

The Dream

The dream began almost as soon as I closed my eyes for the night. Vanessa, your name in this dream, waited with her lovely hair braided, spinning the end of it at me. She said she had stayed clear of mud this time, but that she still ran through the back meadow nude and had plenty of the woods on her to share with me that was tangled in her hair. We climbed on and filled her little bed, clasping close to each other as we did. When we go to bed together there, we never sleep. Never. Sleep stays at the door.

"Vanessa," I asked, "tell me, whom do you love?"

Instead of speaking she caressed me softly and then slipped her hand between my legs and took hold of my cock, but not gently. Pulling it as she maneuvered down, she hovered over it with her mouth and she said, "You, I know I love you, my dear." Then she looked toward my face and said, "Shut your eyes. I want to be with my lover only!"

"Vanessa," I answered, "can you not see that it is me as well."

"No, you are wrong," she said, "I see that you are out of place here."

"But, but .. ," I stammered.

She rejoined, "I really want only your tool. If you don't shut your lids and mouth I will ask you to leave, without it. Here, take your arms back, and here are your hands . . . ."

And so I was removed from me. My cock was delighted, however!

Thinking

I am thinking of her.
I am waiting for her to arrive.
I'm hoping that I'll make love to her.
I am wondering if I will make love to her
when she arrives.
I am curious if she knows what goes on in my mind
when she arrives.

Some Office Work

"Ian, that was nice of you to get the dry cleaning. So how was the rest of your day? Still having a 'bad day'?" I coyly say.

"I'm having a wonderful day," you murmur gently, a soft breathiness coloring your voice.

"Wait till you see what kind of NIGHT you're going to have!" I taunt.

"UH oh," you smile in response.

"Oh, wait!" I sigh. I forgot. I brought home some work from the office that I have to get to before tomorrow. Review sheets and assignments that should completed before 9:00 AM. Why don't I clean up this stuff from dinner, and I'll get started on that work. You could go relax, read the paper, or watch TV or something. Sorry sweetheart, it's just an hour or so of reading. I'll make it up to you later if you are patient."

You sigh as well, but smile when you detect the mischievous sparkle in my eyes. "The night is not yet over," you think to yourself.

I begin to pick up my clothes in preparation to dress, and feel your hand on my arm. "No honey, don't put those back on.," you say. "Go put on that red and black thing, you know, the one with the black lace trim and those little red ties down the front."

"Honey, my work...." I whisper, an anxious look on my face.

"I promise to leave you alone until your work is done. YOU let me know when you are ready to play.   I'm going to go take a shower and then sit down and read the paper or watch TV till you finish."

After you shower, you come into the living room looking for me. Your eyes travel around the room until you see me reclining on the couch. I'm unaware of your presence in the doorway and this gives you a moment to look at me.

I did put on the red teddy with the black lace trim. It's bright red like the dress I had on earlier and has black lace around the French cut legs, and where it dips down to a V in the front just below my waist. It's almost tied closed with the three little red ties in the front.

From where you are standing, you can see the gentle swell of my breasts above the black lace, as I breathe steadily, intent on my work. The notes I'm holding are resting on my stomach just below my breasts, and I'm slowly turning the pages as I read.

You enjoy watching the subtle movement of my breasts as I lift my arm to turn the page. The light above my head shines on my hair which is flowing freely on the pillow and around my shoulders.

You walk over and kneel beside me on the floor and gently lift a curl which is resting on my upper chest. I feel the hair on the back of your hand barely brush against my skin. I sigh and turn my face towards you.

You are twirling the golden curl in your fingers now, feeling its silkiness. I watch your face as your eyes travel the length of my body, enjoying how I feel as I see you look at me. Your finger lightly traces a pattern down the line of skin showing between the ties, and then around the lace at the top of my legs, until you can touch the wisps of hair framing the lace on either side of my teddy.

"How much work do you have, honey?" you ask with barely concealed impatience.

"About a half hour more. Maybe a little less if I can concentrate. It's hard to think when I'm wearing this thing!!" I laugh. "All I can think about is when you are going to take it off me."

"No honey," you say. "I'm going to let you read. I'll wait till you finish."

You walk away and settle in a chair nearby, rustling the newspaper as you bury yourself behind it. I look at you for a moment, sitting there behind that newspaper. All I can see are your legs, and I think about having them wrapped around me when you are deep inside me. I sigh and turn back to my reading. I'm so intent on my reading, I don't hear you get up and go into the kitchen. But when you return, you stop by the couch again, and ask me, "Want a bite of ice cream?"

"In a minute. Let me finish this page." You settle back in your chair with a slightly disdainful look on your face.

"What a NIGHT I'm gonna have?" you question.

"Newspapers, TV, ice cream!"

You set the ice cream down a bit too loudly on the table next to you and pick up the paper again, and rustle it loudly as well, trying to convey your impatience to me.

I smile as I close the notebook and silently cross the room and kneel down in front of you. I lightly trail my fingernails from your ankles to your knees, parting your legs slightly until I can rest between them. Peeking under the newspaper, I smile up at you sweetly and say pleadingly, "Ian, I want my ice cream now!"

You drop the paper to the floor and pick up the bowl and spoon a big bite of ice cream and hold it out in front of me, until I open my mouth to take it. But the ice cream is melting fast and some runs down my chin and drops on your stomach, and you flinch when the coldness hits you.

You laugh as you wipe the ice cream off my chin with your fingers. I grab your hand and slowly lick each finger, up and down, seeking the sweetness of the ice cream with the tip of my tongue, and then circling your palm until the stickiness is all gone, looking at you suggestively while I do this.

Then I look at the ice cream on your stomach, which is starting to drip down towards the waistband of your shorts. I lick it up with just the tip of my tongue, and then move my tongue delicately across your waist until I feel you squirm just a little.

I lick my way up the center of your stomach and then over to each of your nipples, swirling my tongue around until they become hard. Then I sit back a bit and ask, "Are you getting impatient over here sweetheart?"

"Hmmph" you groan. "There is a limit to my patience, DARLING!"

My hands are idly stroking your sides, moving across your upper chest, down the center of your stomach. My stomach is resting against your lap. I can feel the evidence of your desire beginning to stir and press against my body, feeling your heat through the thin satin fabric.

"Just ten more minutes, sweetheart, I promise."

"Oh you! You tease! Just for that!!" You tug gently on the first tie, which loosens quickly and easily, knowing full well the effect this gesture will have on me, as I feel the fabric release its hold on my breasts. My nipples grow taut and press against the wisp of clothing yet covering me, seeking freedom and your touch. You smile teasingly and whisper huskily, "Back to your reading HONEY. I wouldn't think of interrupting you for the next ten minutes!"

Now its my turn to mumble and sigh! "Hmph!"

We both know that this playful game of taunting and teasing is only intensifying and mounting our anticipation and excitement.

When I return to the couch, with my back to you, I slowly and deliberately bend down to punch my pillow just so, and pick up my notebook, knowing full well that you are watching every movement. I can almost feel your loving caress as your gaze moves down my back, follows the curve of my hip, and rests on my scantily clad bottom, before I turn and open my notebook and settle down once again.

I lay with my knees bent, one resting against the back of the couch, and the other idly moving up and down, again absorbed in my work and totally unaware of the effect my unconscious movement is having on you.

The teddy is cut high above the legs, and each time I swing my leg outward, you catch a fleeting glimpse of my reddish hair framed against the narrow strip of black lace running between my legs.

I try to concentrate for about five minutes, but my thoughts are wandering and are no longer on the words on the page. I sigh, and let the notebook drop to the floor and close my eyes a moment, savoring the feel of anticipation.

Unconsciously, and with my eyes still closed, I touch my fingertips to my neck, and stroke along my collarbone, turning my face to one side. As my hand moves down over my shoulders, I spread my fingers and trace light patterns, moving lower, till my hand comes to rest on my left breast, and I massage until the nipple is hard in my palm.

I sigh, open my eyes, and am startled when I notice you watching me with an intensity that bespeaks your own excitement. I move as if to get up, embarrassed, but you cross the room to me, speaking gently in a whisper, "Don't stop honey. Let me watch you."

"I can't. I want YOU Ian." You sit beside me and undo the second tie on my teddy and pick up my own hand and place it over my breast.

"I know you do, but I'd like to watch you." Your hand is softly touching my other breast, until the nipple grows swollen between your fingers. You move your hand over my body, down between my legs and massage the palm of your hand against my mound as I slightly part my legs.

You lift me from the couch and carry me into the bedroom, gently laying me on my back in the center of the bed as you sit beside me. You whisper softly, "You know how much I like to look at your beautiful body."

I nod slowly, a bit reluctantly.

"Don't you like how you feel when I look at you?" You untie the last restraining tie on the front of my teddy and ease the fabric apart, exposing my breasts as you speak, and letting your eyes roam freely, touching each part of me only with the intensity of your gaze. I shudder as I feel a familiar spasm between my legs, and moan softly.

"Yes Ian," I say. "Yes, yes!"

"Relax, dear. Think of me watching you. I know it excites you, and it will excite me. It will excite me to see you touch yourself."

You slowly pull the fabric back over my breasts. Then, taking my hand in yours, you kiss each fingertip and place my hand over my waist. You move across the room and murmur, "Honey, I love you."

I tentatively, hesitantly move one hand over my body, from my waist and over one breast on the outside of my teddy. I pause, uncertain. I touch my right hand to the right side of my neck, and slowly rake my fingernails over the skin, between my chin and my collarbone, rolling my head to one side on the pillow.

I close my eyes, and begin to abandon myself to the sensations of my own hands caressing my body. My thoughts drift to a vision of you watching me, imagining your reaction, imagining your dick growing harder and harder as you see every sign of my mounting passion in a way you have never witnessed before.

My other hand moves up the center of my stomach, touching the skin revealed in the opening of my teddy, and I push the fabric apart further and slide the straps down my shoulders.

I arch my back until the wisp of lace and satin is pushed down around my waist. My hands travel up the length of my body and rest over each breast, cupping them, massaging and caressing, working the nipples into hard peaks.

My breath is coming faster as my excitement mounts, and I am lost to this thing I am doing for you. I open my legs slightly and move one hand down, working it under the fabric until I can feel my own wetness.

I open my legs wider and slide my hand down further, burying my fingertips in my hair which is tangled now and damp from my excitement. I thoroughly wet my finger and then move it up across my body until I can touch each nipple with my wetness, feeling each one grow harder.

I then touch the same finger to my lips and stroke it gently back and forth until I can taste my own saltiness. I open my legs yet wider and stroke my fingertips back and forth across my inner thighs, lightly brushing over the place between my legs. I'm breathing heavy now, and sighing, seemingly forgetting that you are in the room. But I speak your name, "Ian?"

"Yes, dear, I'm here." I can hear a husky, straining sound in your voice as your speak. "Take the teddy off now. Let me see all of your beautiful body."

I slowly arch my back and slide the offending cloth down my hips, until I can kick it off with the motions of my legs.

I bend my legs but hold my knees together, uncertain what to do next. I part my legs slightly and place a hand over my hair, feeling the wetness against my palm.

"Open them wider. Let me see all of you. Lose yourself again honey...for me."

Your voice betrays your own mounting passion and desire, and gives me courage. I allow my legs to drop fully open and begin to explore the soft folds between my legs, easing myself open, pushing the hair aside to allow my fingertip to slide easily between my opening and the swollenness of my clitoris point.

I move my fingertip up and down between my legs, sliding gently with my wetness now evenly distributed, and pausing each time as I touch my clitoris, circling it slowly, enjoy the waves of sensation which are beginning to take hold of me.

My other hand continues to stroke my upper body, across my lower stomach, and up over each breast. I shiver and moan as the first sensation of orgasm begins to wash over me. I place a finger inside my opening, feeling the softness and warmth deep within myself.

"Aaaaahhhhhh" I sigh, as I withdraw my finger and again circle my clitoris. It is hard and erect and each gentle touch brings me closer to climax, yet I try to hold off, allowing the tension to mount. I again move both hands over my upper body, allowing my legs to remain open like a blatant invitation, touching my nipples with my wet finger, and feeling myself shiver.

As I return my hand between my legs, I reinsert a finger and thrust my hips upward, gently rocking in the motions of lovemaking, and slide my finger back up until I can feel my orgasm begin. My finger circles my clitoris with a new intensity and my cries fill the room.

I'm so lost now, I'm unaware that you have joined me on the bed until I can feel your tongue mingle with my own finger, licking and caressing and pushing me over the edge. You push two fingers deep inside me and slowly move them in and out as your tongue continues to probe and touch my pulsing flesh.

"Ian...oooohhhhhhhhhh, yes...I WANT you now. FUCK ME NOW!!!!!!"

My orgasm slowly subsides, and you move between my legs and place your cock just barely inside me. I encircle your flesh with my hand, feeling its length and hardness. I move it up and down between my legs, moaning each time it passes over my still erect clitoris as the last sensations of orgasm die away.

"Ian, you are SO hard!! I want you inside me. Fill me with your cock. FUCK ME!!!"

Your cock moves again to my opening and you thrust gently, pushing a few inches within my warmth and wetness, slowly sliding in. I tighten my muscles against you, trying to pull you deeper inside, moaning again, "FUCK me, fuck me."

You thrust harder, burying yourself deep within me, and I arch upward to meet you, wrapping my legs around your hips. We move in unison, softly moaning with each thrust which brings us closer and you deeper within me.

You are hard like never before, filling me and pounding into me. Each time you thrust deep inside me, I can feel your balls slap against me with the intensity of your movements. Your tongue finds its way into my mouth, seeking mine, until they meet with an urgency equal to the thrusting of our lower bodies.

"Ian...ohhhhhhh...now, COME inside me now. I'm there....COME with me. Oh Ian!"

You can feel the spasms deep within me as I sigh and call your name. Our tongues meet again in a wet, fiery embrace. You tense, and I can feel your cock grow yet harder as you begin to come with an intensity that leaves us both weak and breathless.

Your cum fills me with each deep thrust, until you collapse against me, whispering my name, mingling the dampness of our bodies together as we are still joined.

You tilt your face towards mine until our lips meet in a gentle, soft kiss, and we stay this way awhile, enjoying the sensation of being locked together, feeling our heartbeats against one another and the feel of you within me.
"Oh Ian, I love you." I push the damp hair from your forehead, touch your cheek and kiss you gently again.

"I love you too, dear." You roll off me and pull me into your arms and we settle against each other, allowing our hearts and breathing to slow.

I think about my work. Did I finish it? Who cares!

Right Now

I'm fucking you
Against the chair right now.
Halfway through our meal,
I couldn't wait anymore.

I'm fucking you
Because your jeans were so round
And your top was so tight,
Because of the lipstick you wore.

I'm fucking you
As if my loins were on fire,
And you can only save me,
You with your blouse on the floor.

I'm cuming right now,
And all my senses have stopped,
And my breath has stopped,
You are desire's reservoir!

You

The next poem I write
Will be solemn and serious,
I promised myself.

Then you entered my mind,
With your sensual eyes,
And your stirring lips,
And made a witty, irreverent,
immodest remark.

All the seriousness left,
and my mind thought of you;
only you alone.
And you are never
solemn and serious.

There Again

I am there again,
between your thighs
and so glad again.

Your pubic hairs
are shorter now
and criss-crossed
like golden honeycomb
as I move closer, closer,
and smell your sweet pollen
and wild, raw honey smell.

I open your thighs
and release a sigh
of delight and pride
that I am so welcome there.

I kiss your belly
before moving down
to between your legs;
Slowly,
slowly,
ever so slowly,
kissing each part of you
that has become
so familiar to me
and so close to me

as to almost be a part of me.

Your breathing comes
in huffs and sighs.
It has no cadence now,
as my tongue finds
each sensitive spot
again and again,
again and again,
as I hold your body tight.

Has honey ever tasted thus?
Has a scent ever been so much?

An essence that mingles
the muskiness
of your perfumed body
with the scent
of your sexual urge,
growing stronger,
and more enthralling,
that seems to be calling me
to my primal home.

Slowly,
I go ever slowly
and lighten my touch
if your breath speeds up.
Easy,
I go easy
not to have you race
or have you cum too soon
(there is time for that,
so much time for that).

We're floating,
and falling

and drifting
somewhere
between the earth and the moon.
I am connected to you
and you are connected to me
like we can never be separated.

I kiss your breast,
then the other breast,
then I return again
to between your thighs
another time
to your golden honeycomb
that is my sweet connection to you.

You moan softly
as I move my tongue around
touching every part that brings
motion to your eyes.

I take us both
beyond the places
that we have been before,
and then back again.

And I see it all
in your eyes!

You And Me

We both sit in the dark and are also unenlightened, waiting for a guide to direct us and correct us, as we aim for our dreams.

But where we go, what we'll do and when we know we have found it grows more difficult as we get older.

The era of "I know that," or "I know how" is over, and is replaced by the increasing sense of how little we know as we grow older and gain more and more wisdom.

I invite you to lie down with me and never tell you what I wish of you. We lie completely naked. I with my pride and you with your dignity.

I want to touch and you want to talk. I stroke and lick, and you talk. I want you to cum before I do. You don't, and continue on. Again and again.

How long do I hold out before I cum on my own?

Then I would be guilty of not making love, but only satisfying desire.

My head between your legs goes on for so long.

Do you really want me to be there so long?

Do you want me to know you that well?

The longer I remain, the less I know you. You can smash my dreams with your legs.

"Did you cum?" Naturally, I know.

Although a lie is sometimes more truth-telling than the truth.

You tell the truth.

When

In the mind
I meditate if I shall ever find
release
from this desire that devours me.

So intense is my growing hunger
insatiable at times, I can only wonder
when will
I fully know its hold on me.

I think of you and fantasize,
all my desires I realize,
but held
in this spell of witchery.

I can feel your raging fire,
My body aches with fierce desire
craving
your sweet mastery over me.

In the inner niches of my private mind
I know I shall never find
release,
but that will be so heavenly!

Limerick # 3

There once was a maid with blond flowing hair,
Who decided one day to run fully bare.
She went out quite pristine,
Without even sunscreen,
And came back sunburned everywhere!

Limerick # 4

There once was a lady who came,
So often that it gave her some fame.
When asked why she did it,
She said, "I'll admit it,
I wanted some talent to claim."

About The Author

Iris Mede And Ian Lewis

They are both award-winning authors of short stories, flash fiction and poetry. Their fiction has been published online and in print by amazon.com. They also co-authored collections of short stories and poetry.